Daddy and Papa's Little Angels

Acceptance of All Kinds of People

Written by Mystique Ann U'Nique

Illustrations by Jackie Crofts

AuthorHouse™
1663 Liberty Drive
Bloomington, IN 47403
www.authorhouse.com
Phone: 1-800-839-8640

Published by AuthorHouse 12/20/2013

ISBN: 978-1-4918-4606-3 (sc)
ISBN: 978-1-4918-4723-7 (e)

Library of Congress Control Number: 2013923122

Any people depicted in stock imagery provided by Thinkstock are models, and such images are being used for illustrative purposes only.
Certain stock imagery © Thinkstock.

This book is printed on acid-free paper.

Because of the dynamic nature of the Internet, any web addresses or links contained in this book may have changed since publication and may no longer be valid. The views expressed in this work are solely those of the author and do not necessarily reflect the views of the publisher, and the publisher hereby disclaims any responsibility for them.

authorHOUSE®

Introduction

This children's book was inspired by Elton John's concern over his son Zachary having two homosexual dads. This book was written to promote love and compassion for homosexual families, those living with AIDS, and those who choose to have children via surrogacy. I also wrote to encourage older people who choose to start families. I wrote this book to help take away any related stigmas.

This book is dedicated to Elton John and his partner, David Furnish.
This book is also dedicated to all children of same-sex couples.

Acknowledgments

I would like to thank the AuthorHouse editorial department for proofreading, editing, and making suggestions to my book. I especially thank Amanda Carmichael in the editorial department for assisting me with editing. When people go out of their way to override adjustments to my manuscript even after all adjustment opportunities have been closed, I have to give them recognition. I am grateful for Amanda's professionalism, knowledge, and suggestions in editing. I really appreciated her feedback and reviews of my manuscript. It is a pleasure to have her assigned to assist me with my books.

Next I would like to thank the people of the illustration department for their creativity in the artwork and design of this book. Special thanks goes to Teri Watkins, my book design consultant, for her remarkable knowledge, creativity, suggestions, and skills in the unique design of my books.

Also I would like to thank my publishing consultant, Leandro McMont, who went out of his way to get my illustration package upgraded so that my book would have the finest details. Leandro went even further, requesting a discount on top of the upgrade on my behalf. His act of kindness meant a lot to me, because this children's book was inspired by Elton John; therefore, I wanted to make sure it would be of the very best quality. Thanks, Leandro McMont.

And finally I thank the Elton John AIDS Foundation for all of the work it is doing to help people living with AIDS. One hundred percent of royalty proceeds for this book will be donated to the Elton John AIDS Foundation.

Once upon a time, there lived a little boy named Gabriel. Gabriel lived with his daddy and papa. Daddy and Papa taught Gabriel to have love and compassion for all kinds of people and that it's okay to be different.

Gabriel loved watching his daddy sing and play the piano. Gabriel would climb onto the piano chair and try to play the piano just like his daddy.

Breakfast time was always fun and playful. Gabriel loved to eat the foods his daddy and papa were eating. Gabriel would eat the boiled egg off of his daddy's plate, and his daddy would eat the pineapple off of Gabriel's plate. Papa laughed as he watched Daddy and Gabriel eat off of each other's plate.

Gabriel loved how his papa played airplane with him. Gabriel also enjoyed sitting on his papa's shoulders and going for walks on the beach.

Daddy and Papa often visited the children's hospital and donated money to help children who were sick from diseases like cancer, hemophilia, or AIDS. One of Gabriel's little friends was in that hospital. His name was Michael.

Michael had AIDS, but because Daddy and Papa taught Gabriel to have love and compassion for all kinds of people, Gabriel still enjoyed playing with Michael as if nothing was wrong.

Daddy and Papa invited Michael and his family on a trip to Disneyland with Gabriel.

They all had so much fun. Through their example, Daddy and Papa taught Gabriel that just because someone has AIDS, that does not mean anyone should treat that person any differently. Michael was very happy people still wanted to be his friend even though he had a disease.

Daddy and Papa took Gabriel on a vacation with their friends. Gabriel got to play with other children who had two daddies or two mommies. Two of Daddy and Papa's special friends were named Graham and Arthur. Graham and Arthur had a little boy named Gus and a little girl named Dee. Gabriel was happy because he had something in common with other children who had two daddies just like him. Papa put a life jacket on Gabriel and took him on a fun boat ride.

Gabriel was very happy. On the beach, Gabriel played in the sand and made sand castles.

Daddy and Papa wanted to make their son happy and safe.

After a long day at the beach, it was time to come home. After Daddy and Papa gave Gabriel a bath and dressed him in his favorite pajamas, Gabriel crawled happily into bed because he knew it was story time. Gabriel loved story time.

At bedtime, Daddy and Papa read Gabriel his favorite stories.

"Papa, will you please read me this book?" Gabriel asked, pointing to a book called *It's Okay to Be Different*. Papa smiled at Gabriel and grabbed the book off the shelf. As Gabriel happily listened, Papa began to read.

"It's okay to be different. Some people are tall, and some people are short. Some people are big, and some people are small. Some people have long hair, some people have short hair, and some people have no hair.

"It's okay to be different. Some people can see, and some people cannot see. Some people can hear, and some people cannot hear. Some people have two arms or two legs, and some people have one arm or one leg.

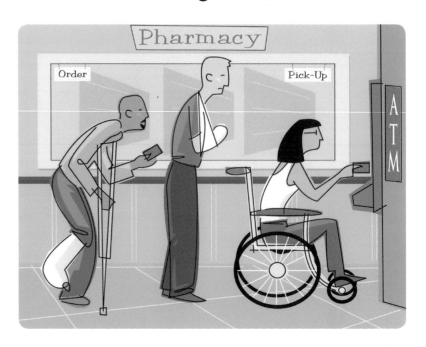

"It's okay to be different. Skin color comes in many colorful shades. Some people have dark skin, and some people have light skin. Some people have straight hair, and some people have curly hair. Some people have hair that feels like silk, and some people have hair that feel like wool.

People have all have different shapes and sizes of noses, eyes, lips, hands, and ears.

"It's okay to be different. The end."

Gabriel was very happy. "Daddy, will you please read me a story?"

Daddy smiled and said, "Yes, I will." As Papa tucked Gabriel into bed, Daddy grabbed a book off the shelf called *We Are Family*. Daddy began to read.

"Some children live with a daddy and a mommy and are very happy.

Some children live with a grandmother and a grandfather and are very happy.

Some children live with an aunt and an uncle and are very happy. Some children live with one mommy and are very happy.

Some children live with one daddy and are very happy.

Some children live with a big sister or brother and are very happy. Some children live with two mommies and are very happy.

Some children live with two daddies and are very happy.

It does not matter who you live with or what their skin color is, because you are all family. It does not matter if you were adopted, because you are all family. Love is what is most important to be a real family.

The end."

Little Gabriel smiled and smiled. "Papa, now will you please read me another story?"

Papa smiled and went to the shelf to get little Gabriel's other favorite story, *The Gift*. As Papa sat down with the book, Gabriel was excited. Papa began to read.

"Once upon a time on a beautiful spring day on a farm, everyone was celebrating all of their new babies. Mr. and Mrs. Pig had new babies, Mr. and Mrs. Cow had a new baby, and Mr. and Mrs. Sheep had a new baby.

"Down by the lake, families of ducks were also celebrating because of their newly hatched eggs. The duck families were all happy, except for Mrs. Daisy and her husband, Bernie Duck.

Year after year, Daisy and Bernie watched all of their friends celebrate the arrival of their new babies. But poor Daisy Duck was unable to lay eggs. The other ducks had compassion for Daisy and Bernie Duck. "One day, while Daisy and Bernie Duck were sitting under a tree having a nice picnic, several of their duck friends came over smiling. Daisy and Bernie wondered what this was all about. Then Mrs. Ivy Duck took out a basket from behind her back and handed it to Daisy and Bernie.

Daisy and Bernie took the basket and looked inside, where they found six eggs.

"Daisy and Bernie smiled with tears in their eyes. 'This is a gift to you,' said Ivy Duck. 'Six duck families each gave you an egg from their nests so you could have a family of your own.' Daisy and Bernie thanked their friends for their love and compassion. Everyone celebrated as Daisy and Bernie built a

nest. Daisy sat on her eggs to keep them nice and warm.

"When the time came for her eggs to hatch, Daisy and Bernie were blessed with six little ducklings.

They would never forget the love and compassion their friends had for someone who could not have babies of her own. This was a gift of love. And they lived happily ever after."

Papa looked at Gabriel and saw that he was fast asleep. As Papa put the books back on the shelf, Daddy gave Gabriel a good-night kiss on his cheek. Daddy and Papa quietly walked to the door and looked back at Gabriel and smiled, because they would never forget that a kind woman once gave her egg to them as a gift so they could have little Gabriel.

Gabriel's New Baby Brother

Daddy and Papa wanted Gabriel to have someone to play with so he would never be alone. One beautiful day, Daddy and Papa got wonderful news from the hospital. It was time for Gabriel's new baby brother to come home. Gabriel was very happy and excited to finally meet his new baby brother. The woman who had been kind enough to give Daddy and Papa their first gift of love so they could have Gabriel also gave them a second gift of love, Raphael.

Gabriel loved his baby brother very much. He was very protective of him. As little Raphael got older, Daddy and Papa took him on a fun boat ride with Gabriel. He wore his life jacket just like Gabriel. Gabriel taught his little brother how to make sand castles. Raphael loved his big brother very much.

Daddy and Papa wanted to teach Raphael how to play the piano like they taught Gabriel. Raphael was too little to play the big piano like Gabriel, so Daddy and Papa bought Raphael a little piano just his size. Raphael wanted to be just like his big brother, so when he saw Daddy giving Gabriel his piano lessons, Raphael watched and played his little piano too.

Christmastime was always fun and exciting. Gabriel and Raphael helped Daddy and Papa decorate the Christmas tree. Gabriel and Raphael's favorite Christmas present was the swing set they received for the garden.

During music time, Daddy sat at the piano and played music and sang songs. He sang Gabriel a song called "Zip-a-Dee-Doo-Dah" but changed it to "Gabriel-A-Dee-Doo-Dah." He sang, "Gabriel-a-dee-doo-dah, Gabriel-a-dee-ay, my oh my, what a wonderful day! Plenty of sunshine heading my way, Gabriel-a-dee-doo-dah, Gabriel-a-dee-ay!"

Next Daddy sang Raphael a song called "Delilah" but changed it to "Raphael." He sang, "I saw the light on the night that I passed by her window. I saw the flickering shadows of love on her blind. She was my woman. As she deceived me, I watched and went out of my mind. My, my, my Raphael, why, why, why, Raphael …"

On a nice, sunny day, Daddy and Papa went on another family trip with their friends Graham and Arthur and their two children, who loved playing with Gabriel and Raphael. Everyone went on boat rides and out to eat and took pictures. Daddy and Papa looked forward to taking a family vacation with Graham and Arthur every year. Everyone was happy.

After a fun day out, it was time for Gabriel and Raphael to come home again and get ready for story time. After taking baths and getting into their pajamas, Gabriel and Raphael went to the bookshelf to get some of their favorite books. Raphael got the book called *Hungry Caterpillar and Stick Man*. Gabriel got the book called *The Gruffalo*. Daddy and Papa sat down with Gabriel and Raphael and each read

them a book. Daddy read *Hungry Caterpillar and Stick Man*. Then Papa read *The Gruffalo*.

Gabriel smiled and said, "Papa, will you please read *The Gift*?"

"Okay, one more book, and then it's time for bed," Papa said.

Gabriel and Raphael said, "Yay!"

As Papa went to get Gabriel's favorite book, Daddy tucked the boys into bed.

When Papa was finished reading, he looked at Gabriel and Raphael and saw that they were fast asleep. Papa looked at Daddy and smiled. As Daddy put all of the books back onto the shelf, Papa gave Gabriel and Raphael gentle kisses on their little cheeks. Then Daddy walked over, kneeled down, and gave Gabriel and Raphael smooches on their tiny cheeks too.

They were very happy because they would never forget when a kind woman gave her eggs to them as a gift so they could have Gabriel and now little Raphael too.

"You and the boys have made my life happier than ever," Daddy said to Papa. "I love you."

Papa smiled back. "Thanks. I love you too."

They gave each other a big bear hug and silently left the room.

The end

CPSIA information can be obtained
at www.ICGtesting.com
Printed in the USA
393836LV00001B/2

* 9 7 8 1 4 9 1 8 4 6 0 6 3 *